ديباك وعيد الديوالي

Deepak's Diwali

Divya Karwal

Illustrated by Doreen Lang

Arabic translation
by Wafa' Tarnovska

Mantra Lingua

في ليلة قبل عيد الديوالي حكى دادي لديباك قصة راما وزوجته سيتا.

وصف دادي ملك العفاريت راڤانا وكيف انه اختطف سيتا.

The night before Diwali, Dadi told Deepak the story of Rama, and his wife, Sita. Dadi described the demon king, Ravana, and how he stole Sita away.

"كان لراقُنا عشرة رؤوس وعشرون أعين تلمع،" تابع دادي بصوت منخفض. اختبأ ديباك تحت الأغطِية.

"Ravana, with his ten heads and twenty flashing eyes," Dadi continued, in a hushed voice. Deepak hid under the covers.

عند الفطور، لم يتمكن ديباك أن يكف عن التفكير في القصة.

"لا تقلق يا ديباك،" قال الأب. "هل تعلم أن راما وصيدقه هانومان،
القرد المقاتل، انتصروا على راڤانا في النهاية."

At breakfast, Deepak couldn't stop thinking about the story.
"Stop worrying, Deepak," said Dad. "You know Rama and his
friend Hanuman, the monkey warrior, beat Ravana in the end."

شعَرَ ديباك بالتحسّن قليلاً الى أن قال له أبوه أنّهُ لَم يستطَعْ أن يشتري القضبان النارية لحفلة الليلة.

إنَّ القضبان النارية هي أفضل جزء من احتفالات عيد الديوالي بالنسـبة لديباك.

Deepak felt a bit better, until Dad told him that he hadn't been able to buy any sparklers for the party that evening. Sparklers were Deepak's favourite part of Diwali.

"ماذا بك؟" سأله صديقه الحميم تيم، وهما على طريق المدرسة.

"هذا أسوأ عيد ديوالي في حياتي،" تنهّد ديباك. "لم يستطع والدي أن
يحصل على القضبان النارية، كما أن أضواء الزينة معطّلة، ثم أني
أخشى أنّ راڤانا ملك العفاريت يطاردني."

"What's wrong Deepak?" asked his best friend, Tim, on the way to school.
"It's the worst Diwali *ever*," Deepak sighed. "Dad couldn't get any sparklers,
the fairy lights aren't working and, even worse," he whispered, "I think
Ravana, the demon king, is after me."

"هذا غير مضحك،" قال ديباك بينمــــا حاولَ تيم أن لا يضحك. "انه هناك."

لكنهما عندما نظرا الى الوراءِ لم يستطيعا رؤية أي شيء.

"هيّا يا فتيان، سنتأخّر،" قالت الام.

"It's not funny," said Deepak, as Tim tried to keep a straight face. "He's just there." But when they looked over their shoulders they couldn't see anything. "Come on boys, we'll be late," said Mum.

"هل رافَقَنا مازال يطارِدُكَ؟" سألَ تيم مبتسماً.

"لا أستطيع رؤيته،" أجابَ ديباك متطّلعاً الى الوراء.

كان تيم معتاداً على حكايات ديباك الخيالية لكنه رأى أن ديباك كان غير راضٍ.

"لا تقلَقْ يا ديباك، لدينا عددٌ كبيرٌ من القضبان النارية استعداداً للإحتفال بليلة غاي فوكْس، يمكنُكَ أن تستعيرَ بعضاً مِنها إذا أرَدْتَ."

"Is Ravana still chasing you?" said Tim, smiling.
"I can't see him," said Deepak, looking over his shoulder.
Tim was used to Deepak's wild stories, but he could see he was upset.
"Don't worry Deepak, we've got lots of sparklers ready for Guy Fawkes Night,
you can borrow some if you like."

"شكراً يا تيم،" أجابَ ديباك. "سأطلب من أمّي أن تُخيط لَكَ أحْسَن زي لحفلةِ المدرسةِ هذه السنةِ. انا ذاهِبٌ كقرصانٍ." كان ديباك فخوراً بالأزياء التي كانت تخيطها أمُه. "من ستكون؟"

"من الأرجح أني سأكون روبين هود،" قالَ تيم.

"Thanks, Tim," said Deepak. "I'll ask Mum to make you the best costume ever for the school party this year. I'm going as a pirate." Deepak was proud of his mum's costumes. "Who are you going to be?"
"I think I'll be Robin Hood," said Tim.

لم يظهّرْ راڤانا على طريق العودَةِ الى البيتِ، وكَادَ دِيباكَ ينساهُ عندما دعَسَ فوق زخارف الرانغولي الملوّنْة المرسومة على عتبة بيته. لقد كانَ قدْ رسمَها معَ امهِ البَارحَهَ لاستقبالِ الضيوف.

There was no sign of Ravana on Deepak's way home, and he had nearly forgotten about him as he stepped carefully over the beautiful Rangoli patterns on his doorstep. He and Mum had made them the night before to welcome the guests.

وجَدَ ديباك ثلاثةَ ظروفٍ حامِلَةً إسمَهُ على ممسحة الأرجل. كانت بطاقاتُ عيد الديوالي من ناني ونانا واولاد عمِهِ بُعِثَتْ من الهندِ.

On the doormat, Deepak found three colourful envelopes addressed to him. They were Diwali cards from Nani and Nana and his cousins, sent all the way from India.

إنَّ الروائح الزكية المنبثقةُ من المطبخ جعلت فمَ ديباك يريّل.

كان هناك السمبوسك وحلويات صفراء ملوّنة اسمها لادو المفضلّة لدى ديباك.

"مرحباً ماما، مرحباً جدّي،" قال ديباك وهو يمدُّ يدَهُ نحو قطعة لادو.

"تمهّل!" قالت الام. "لا يمكننا أكل هذه اللادو قبل أن نقدمها للالهةِ هذا المساء.

كلْ سندويشاً الآن."

The delicious smells coming from the kitchen made Deepak's mouth water.
There were samosas and yellow sweet balls called ladoos, Deepak's favourite.
"Hi Mum, hi Dadi," said Deepak, as he reached for a ladoo.
"Hold on!" said Mum. "We can't eat these ladoos before we offer them to the gods
this evening. Have a sandwich for now."

طلب دبياك اذا كان يستطيع دعوة تيم وابيه للسهرة وفسَّر لأبيهِ قصة القضبان النارية.

"أظنُّ أنه سيكون لديك قضبان نارية إضافية هذه السنة،" أجابَ والداه بغمزَةٍ.

"لدينا أضواءُ زينةٍ جديدة لهذه الليلة."

يظهرُ أن الوضعَ ليس بالسوء الذي تصوّره ديباك.

Deepak asked if Tim and his dad could spend the evening with them and explained about the sparklers.
"You'll have extra sparklers this year," said Dad with a wink. "And we've got some new fairy lights for tonight."
Perhaps things wouldn't be so bad after all.

بدّلَ ديباك ملابسَهُ وأرتدى الكورتا والباجاما التقليديتان، ثم ساعَدَ أمَّهُ وجدّه على إعداد قناديل الزيت.

وضعوا قنديلاً على كل شباك وامام الباب. لكنّ القناديل كانت تُطفأُ دائما بسبب الريح.

Deepak quickly changed into the traditional Kurta-Paijama, and helped Mum and Dadi prepare the oil lamps. They put one on every windowsill and at the front door. But the lamps kept blowing out.

"هذا راڤانا،" قال ديباك.

"إنها ليلةٌ عاصفة، يا ديباك،" أجابت الأم. "سنتركُ أبواب النوافِذ مفتوحةَ كي تصِدَّ الالهةُ لكشمي الارواحَ الشريرةَ، فلا تقْلَقْ!"

"It's Ravana!" said Deepak.
"It's just a windy night, Deepak," said Mum. "We'll leave the doors and windows open for goddess Lakshmi to keep bad spirits away, so no more worrying!"

حانَ وقتُ الصلاةِ. أضاءت الأمُّ قنديلاً أمامَ صورةِ راما، وأخيهِ لاكْشمان، وسيتا، وهانومانْ. حضَّرَت التيكا بمَزْج بودرَةٍ حمراءَ خاصةْ معَ بعضِ الماءَ. ثمَّ وضعتْ علامةَ التيكا على جَبهةِ الجميعِ لَجلْب الحظِّ.

Soon it was time to pray. Mum lit a lamp in front of a picture of Rama, his brother, Lakshman, Sita, and Hanuman. She prepared the tika by mixing special red powder with a few drops of water. She then carefully put a tika on everyone's forehead for good luck.

ثم قدّمتْ العائلةُ حَلْوى اللادوزْ الى الاِلِهة. ثمَّ رنَّموا صلاةَ الآرتي مادحين راما وشاكرينه بركته وَمنحه السلامِ والسعادةِ للجميعْ. لم يستطَعْ ديباكْ الانتظارْ بعدْ، فأكَلَ إحدَى قطَعِ الحلوى اللذيذةِ بشراهةٍ.

The family offered ladoos to the gods. Then they sang an Aarti praising Rama and thanking him for blessing everyone with happiness and peace. Deepak couldn't resist any more and gobbled down one of the delicious sweets.

"هيا نُكَلِّمْ جدتُكَ جدُكَ ناني ونانا،" قالَ الأبَ. "لقد قرُبتْ الساعة الثانية عشرة ليلاً في الهندِ لكنهما ساهران خصّيصاً."

"Let's call Nani and Nana," suggested Dad. "It's nearly midnight in India but they're staying up especially."

"كلُّ ديوالي وانتِ سالمةٍ، ناني! كلُّ ديوالي وانتَ سالمٍ، يا نانا!"
"وانتَ سالَم أيضاً يا حفيدَنا الصغير،" أجاب الجدّان وتمنياً له السعادةَ للسنةِ القادمة. قال ديباك أنَّه اشتَاق لَهما، لكن امَّهُ وَعَدَتْ انهُمْ سيزورونَ الهندَ في كانونِ الأولِ.
ثم قرعَ جَرسُ البابِ.

"Happy Diwali, Nani! Happy Diwali, Nana!"
"And to you, Beta," his grandparents replied and they wished him happiness for the year ahead. Deepak missed them, but Mum promised that they would visit India in December.
Just then the doorbell rang.

"كل ديوالي وأنتُمْ سالِمون!" قالتِ العمّةُ والعَمُّ وابنَةُ العَمِّ تارا وتعانَقَ الجميعُ في المدْخَلِ. ثم قدَّمَتْ العمّةُ علبة حلوى من لونِ القشطةِ على شكل مربعات مُغطاة بورقٍ فضّي. جاءَ تيم أيضاً. جَلَبَ هُوَ وأبوهِ كيساً كلّهُ قضبان نارية. كانَ ديباك ينتظِرُ بفارغِ الصبرِ ان يراها تفرقع وتفور.

"Happy Diwali!" said Aunty and Uncle and cousin Tara, and everyone hugged in the hall. Aunty brought a box of cream coloured sweets, shaped like diamonds with silver paper on top. Tim came too. He and his dad brought a bag full of sparklers. Deepak couldn't wait to set them crackling and fizzing.

كان العشاءُ لذيذاً مكوناً من صحونِ الحُمصِ بالكاري، من جبنةِ البانير، من خُبزِ البوري المقليِ، من كمياتٍ كبيرةٍ من الأرزِ المعطَّرِ بالكمّونِ ومن الحلاوةِ اللذيذةِ.

"أظنُّ أنَّ راقآنا سينتقَمُ هذه الليلةِ،" قالَ ديباك هازئاً. "أظنُّ أنَّهُ سيسرُقُ تارا لكيْ تأخُذَ مكان سيتا التي فقَدَها."

"ليجرّب!" صاحت تارا بعنفٍ.

"ديباك! كفْ عن تخويفِ ابنةِ عمّكَ،" قالت الأُم.

"لَسْتُ خائفة!" اجابَتْ تارا، "إني سأقطَعُ كلَّ واحدٍ من رؤوسهِ العَشْرةْ."

"لا أظنّ أنَّ لَديهِ أيُّ حظٍ بالفوزِ ضدَّ تارا،" ضحِكَ العّم.

The meal was delicious, with platefuls of chickpea curry, paneer, fried puree bread, mounds of cumin rice and yummy halwa pudding. "I think Ravana is going to take his revenge tonight," Deepak teased. "I think he's going to steal Tara to make up for losing Sita."

"I'd like to see him try," said Tara fiercely. "Deepak! Stop trying to frighten your cousin," said Mum. "I'm not scared!" said Tara, "I'd chop all ten of his heads off." "I don't think he'd stand much of a chance against Tara," laughed her dad.

بعدَ العشاءِ، فسَّرَت الأمُّ لماذا يُضيُّ الناسُ القناديلَ بمناسبةِ عيدِ الديوالي.

"عندَمَا خلَّصَ راما وهانومان سيتا من قبضَةِ راڤانا، أضاءَ الناسُ

فوانيسَ من الطينِ تُسمَّى "ديباكس"،

وذلك للإحتفالِ بانتِصارِ الحقِّ على الباطِلِ."

"يَعْني انَّ إسمي معناهُ "إحتفال،"" قال ديباك بافتخارٍ.

"او لـَقْكت من الطينِ،" قالت تارا، فضحكَ تيم.

"تعالوا يا أولاد، حانَ وقتُ القضبانِ الناريّةِ!" نادى الأبُ من الحديقَة.

After dinner, Mum explained why people light lamps at Diwali.
"When Rama and Hanuman rescued Sita from Ravana, the people burned clay lamps, called deepaks, to celebrate the triumph of good over evil."
"So my name means celebration," said Deepak proudly.
"Yes, or just a lump of clay," said Tara, making Tim laugh.
"C'mon kids, it's time for sparklers!" Dad called from the garden.

بينما فرقعت وطقطقت القضبان النارية في الظلمَةِ، كانَ ديباك، تيم وتارا يتخيّلونَ أنهُمْ يَرونَ هانومانْ يَتقاتَلُ معَ راڤانا.

As their sparklers sputtered and crackled in the dark, Deepak, Tim and Tara were sure they could see Hanuman fighting Ravana.

"تعالى يا هانومان!" صاحوا جميعاً.

"لنساعِدَه!" صَرَختْ تارا، بينَما كانوا يُلوحونَ بالقضبانِ الناريّةِ، وكأنّهم يتَهجّمونَ على الليل.

"C'mon Hanuman!" they all yelled.
"Let's help!" cried Tara, as they twirled their sparklers, attacking the night.

بعدَ المعركةِ، أكلَ المنتصرونَ اللادوز والبورفيز ليَدْفَؤُن، ثمَّ حانَ وقتُ الرجوعِ الى البيتِ. سألَ ديباك أمَهُ إذا كانتَ تستطيعُ خياطةَ زَيِّ روبين هود لتيم. لكنّ تيم هزَّ برأسِهِ.

After the battle, the victors had ladoos and burfis to warm themselves up, and then it was time to go home. Deepak asked Mum if she would make a Robin Hood costume for Tim, but Tim shook his head.

"لَسَتُ أكيداً أنني أريدُ أنْ أكونَ روبين هود الآن،" قالَ تيم.

"إِذاً،" قالَتِ الأمُّ، "يمكنني أن أُخَيِطَ لَكَ أيّ زيّ تريدُه. قُلْ لي مَن تريدُ أن تكَّون."

"I'm not sure I want to be Robin Hood now," he said.
"Well Tim," said Mum, "I can make any costume you like. Just let me know who you want to be."

"إنني هانومان، القردُ المحارب!" قالَ تيم.

"وأنا راما!" ضحِكَ ديباك.

"I'm Hanuman, the monkey warrior!" said Tim.
"And I am Rama!" laughed Deepak.

Glossary

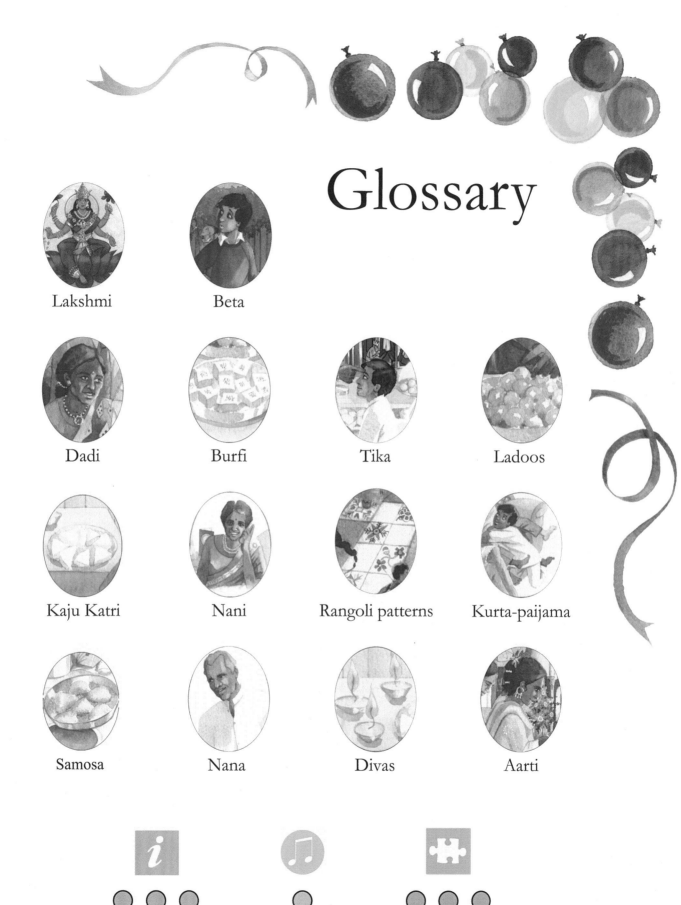

Lakshmi

Beta

Dadi

Burfi

Tika

Ladoos

Kaju Katri

Nani

Rangoli patterns

Kurta-paijama

Samosa

Nana

Divas

Aarti

Recipes

Mango Lassi

Ingredients
175ml yogurt
150ml milk
1 peeled chopped mango
1 tablespoon sugar
1 tablespoon honey
8 ice cubes
A little ground cardamom
or some chopped pistachio
nuts (if you like)

Method
1. Put all the ingredients in a blender and blend for two minutes or until smooth. If you don't have a blender you can use a whisk and add the ice later.
2. Strain through a sieve to remove any large ice chunks and big pieces of mango.
3. Pour into glasses and serve with a dusting of ground cardamom or pistachio nuts.

Halwa

Ingredients
100g sugar
200g water
2 tablespoons unsalted butter
300g carrots, grated
300ml full fat milk
½ tsp powdered cardamom
1 tablespoon of cashew nuts, chopped finely

Method
1. Mix the sugar with double the quantity of water in a heavy saucepan and bring to the boil.
2. Reduce heat and cook until the syrup has thickened slightly. Take off the heat and set aside.
3. In the meantime, heat the butter in a heavy-bottomed saucepan and add the carrots, stirring occasionally to prevent them from sticking.

4. After 5 minutes add the sugary syrup and stir until blended.
5. Pour in the milk, reduce the heat and cook until the carrots are mushy, the milk has been soaked up, and the mixture has turned brown.
6. Take off the heat, mix in the cardamom, and serve warm, decorated with the nuts. Halwa is delicious served with plain yogurt or vanilla ice-cream.

Cooking equipment can be dangerous, so make sure you are always with an adult when preparing food.

i

Kheer

Ingredients   *Method*

Ladoos

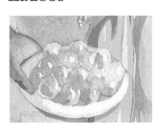

Ingredients   *Method*

Story

Rangoli Patterns

Here are some Rangoli patterns, like the ones that Deepak made for his house.
You can find some special grid paper on our website, *www.mantralingua.com*, so
that you can copy these or make your own patterns.

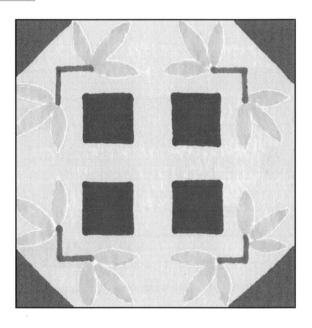

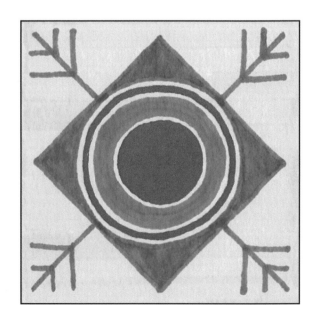